청어詩人選 230

권오정 제7시집
Kwon Oh-jeong's 7th Anthology of Poetry
Anthology of Poetry Korean-English
-한영시집-

꽃과 바람의 노래
The Songs of Flowers & Winds

청어

헛소리

꽃이 좋아
꽃을 그렸습니다

바람이 좋아
바람을 노래했습니다

꽃바람
언덕에 올라
꽃이 되었습니다

꽃 살림 차려놓고
꽃 노래 부르며

꽃 같은 無我之境으로 살다가
사는 것 시들해지면
꽃 편지 써야지

사랑하느라 고달프다고
받기보다 하느라 고달프다고
꽃을…

창조주께서
가장 싫어하는 사람은
사랑이 아까운 사람
가장 좋아하는 사람은
노래하는 사람

다음으로 좋아하는 사람은
그림 그리는 사람
더욱 좋아하는 사람은
노래하고 그리는 사람

다시 돌아오지 못할 멀어져간 날들
오늘 허허함에 어찌할 바를 모르는
그대 가슴에

지금 선 자리에

한순간
마음속 갈잎 피리 소리로 남아
울고 싶은 시인이 있습니다.

Nonsense

As I liked the flowers
I drew the flowers.

As I liked the wind
I sang the wind.

I climbed the hill of spring breeze
And I turned into a flower.

Arranging flowery house
Where I sang the flowers
And I fell into a flowery life with delirious happiness.

And when I'm sick and tired of it,
I will write a flowery letter.

A flowery letter telling that I'm tired
of loving instead of being loved.
The flower⋯

The person disliked most by the Creator
Is the person who spares love.
And the most beloved person is the person who sings
songs.

And the next beloved person is the person
Who draws the picture.
And the more beloved person is the person
Who sings songs and draw pictures.

The days passed far behind of never return
Embarrassed by the empty heart of today
In your heart

Where I stay

One moment,
One poet stays who is apt to weep
Remain as a sound of reed leaf pipe in the heart.

【 차례 】

序詩_헛소리 Nonsense

1부

2부

3부

이기태(李起台)

호: 鹿山
시인, 《문예운동》 등단, 수필가, 번역시인

청하문학회이사, 미국 All Poetry 영어시단회원,
문예운동공동발행인, 한국문인협회인성교육위
부위원장, 서울詩壇회원, 국제PEN한국본부회원.
서울대 총동창회 종신회원

저서:
산문집 『바다, 그 끝없는 유혹』,
시집 『작은별 숲에 머물다』 등 4권,
한·영 대역시집 『부르지 못한 슬픈 노래』 등 5권,
주간한국문학신문에 한·영대역시 4년째 연재 중.

E-mail: kkeystar@hanmail.net

Profile of the 1st Part Translator.
Lee Keytae
Poet, Essayist, Poetry Translator
Member of US All Poetry

Director of the Alumni Association of the
Seoul National University.
Graduated from the Dennis Realty School
in L. A.

Author of 4 books:
A Little Star Nests in the Forest and 3
others
Translated 5 Korean poetry books into
English
Currently translating Korean poems into
English for 4 years in the Weekly Korean
Literature Newspaper.

1부

번역: 이기태

1st Part

Translated by
Lee Keytae

꽃인가 바람인가

영롱한 이슬처럼
웃음 짓기에

살랑이는 몸짓으로
마음 흔들기에

스치는 바람인가 했더니

그 꽃은 서러움이었네
사무치는 그리움이었네

내 가슴에 서리서리 핀
얼음꽃이었네.

Is It Flower or Wind

As it smiled like
The brilliant dews

As it moved my heart
In a dancing gesture

I presumed if it is the brushing wind.

That flower was sorrow
It was a heart-breaking longing.

It was an ice flower
That bloomed coil after coil in my heart.

꽃신

연두빛 물감 흩뿌려
일순에 녹음 산천이라

봄 동산 휘젓고 다니던 햇살은
실개천에 푸른 물 풀어 내리고

복사 빛 짙어져
꽃들이 나를 유혹하는 날
바람난 춘녀春女가 되어

들꽃 화관을 쓰고
하늘빛 푸른 바람에
옷자락 휘날리며

꽃바람 꽃신 신고
강바람 들바람 휘돌아 싸돌아
숨차고 지치면

흐르는 강물 위에
낙화처럼 꽃신을 띄우리라.

Flower Shoes

In a moment, the hills and streams
Became green ones
By spraying light blue paints.

The sunshine whirled around in the spring garden
It dyed the small stream in green.

When the radiant light was thickened
The flowers attracted
And I became a flirtatious spring flapper.

I wore a crown of wild flowers
Fluttering my light skirt
In the wind concerted with the blue sky.

Wearing flower decorated shoes in the spring breeze
The wind from the river and field whirled
And moved around.

When it is hard to breathe and I am tired
I will float in the flower shoes
Like the falling flower in the flowing river.

꽃이여!

고울사 꽃이여!

꽃은 피어
그 누구의 기쁨이 되고
꽃은 피어
그 누구의 슬픔이 되고

꽃 피어
네 가슴에 환희가 넘치고
슬픔 차올라
눈물이야 흐르건 말건

꽃이여!
화사한 빛으로
도도하게 순간을 삼키고
순간을 나르며 영원히 죽더라도

청춘을 꽃다이 날리며
꿈처럼 피고 지는
너는 꽃.

Oh, My Dear Flower!

You are so beautiful, flower!

Flower blooms
To become the joy for someone

Flower blooms
To become the sorrow for someone

Flower blooms
To fill the jubilance for someone
When sadness fills up
You don't care whether I burst into tears or not

Dear flower!
You arrogantly devour the moments
With bright light,
Even though you carry moments and then die forever.

You blow up your youth flowerlike
Blooming and falling like in a dream,
You are a flower.

너 때문에

꽃 너 때문에
오늘 내가 슬프고 외롭다

네 아리따운 꽃 빛
어이 할 수 없어
그 때문에 안타까워

네 애잔한 모습
슬픔 더욱 깊어져
네 파르르한 떨림
가슴 아려와

이 정오의 언덕에서
흐느껴 울고 싶구나

아~ 어쩔거나
이 슬픔
이 상심.

Because of You

Because of you, flower
I am sad and lonely today.

Your beautiful flower color
I can't do anything on this
I feel pitiful about this.

Your sorrowful appearance
Makes my sorrow still deeper,
Your light trembling
Makes my heart hurt.

When the sun is high in the sky at noon
I want to sob.

Ah~ I don't know how I can control
My sadness,
My broken-heart!

목련
－恨

목련이라는 이름의
소복한 여인이여

한 맺힌 소리
하늘 향해 펑펑 쏟아붓고는

저토록 처참히
죽어가는 여인아

무심한 하늘은
그저 말이 없구나

아아！이른 봄
저 탄식의 나날이여

애련으로 피멍 든 자목련
가슴 저린 아픔

견디지 못해
죽고 마는 여인아

아으～ 피맺힌 사연
어느 하늘에 풀어 볼꺼나.

Magnolia
-Resentment

You, a lady
Named Magnolia clad in white

You poured a lot of sound
Of resentment Towards the sky

So terribly
Dying lady

The indifferent sky
Speaks just nothing

Alas! In the early spring
The days of sighs every day

The lily magnolia blooded in pity
Has heartburn pain

You, poor lady can't stand
and finally die

Alas! The bloody stories,
In which corner of the sky
Will you release them?

봄은!

산 넘어
향기 담은 촉수

살큼 살큼 고양이 걸음
동글동글 눈동자 속에 감추고

알싸한 봄소식 어디에 전할까

할미꽃잎 속 숨 고르기
뉘 가슴 사알짝 흩트려 놓을까

사정없이 피는 들꽃에
취한 나그네.

Spring is!

Scented tentacles
Over the hill

Gentle cat's walk
Hides itself in its pupils

To whom shall the spring news be delivered~

It's a taking breath inside the pasque flower petal
Whose heart it shall scatter secretly.

A stranger
Intoxicated by the wild flowers
That's blooming anytime anywhere.

사랑은 그대에게

사랑은 그대에게
한 방울 이슬처럼 왔나요
밤새 핀 꽃잎처럼 왔나요

사랑은 그대에게
향긋한 꽃 향기로 왔나요
꽃 나비 사뿐한 나래로 왔나요

사랑은 그대에게
살랑이는 잎새처럼 왔나요
하롱하롱 내리는 연분홍 꽃이었나요

사랑은 그대에게
불고 간 바람처럼
소리 없이 왔다가 사라졌나요.

2017 가곡 백승태 곡, 김정연 노래

Love for You

Did the love reach you
Like a drop of dew?
Or like petals bloomed all night long?

Did the love reached you
Being a fragrance of the flower?
Or light wings of butterflies~

Did the love reached you
Like the dancing tree leaves
Or the carelessly falling light pink flower~

Did the love reached you
Like the blown wind
With no notice and disappeared~

2017 Composed by Baek Seung Tae, song by Kim Jung Yeon

솔바람 소리

송화 가루 날리는 윤사월
어디선가
들려오는 솔바람 소리

문설주에 기대어
귀 기울이면

쏴~아 하고 밀려오는
파도 소리
불현듯 그리운 바다

솔향기 봄바람 소리에
설레는 마음

꽃바람 손잡고 오는
귀살쩍은 소리.

The Sound of Breeze in Pine Trees

In intercalary April by lunar calendar
when pine pollen dancing
The sound of breeze in pine trees
Is dimly heard from somewhere.

When I listen to it
Leaning on the doorpost

Sound of high sea~
The sound of dashing waves
A sudden missing of the sea.

In the sound of spring breeze of pine scent
My heart flutters.

The cute sound of spring breeze
Is heard coming hand in hand.

자운영 미소

쟁기 밭 이랑 사이 엄동설한에
산고의 아름다움이 자운영이어라

올올이 칼날이여 비수인가
고개 들기 전 그러했으리

봄이 오는 소리 귓가에 스치면
앉은뱅이 들꽃으로 피어나니
베어다 그대 고운 옷 지으리

터진 손 호호 불어 날실 삼고
씨실에 반짝이는 수정은
눈물로 키운 사랑이니

따스한 봄볕 들면
당신의 상처 난 가슴을
자운영 붉은빛으로 어루리이다.

The Smile of Astragalus Sinicus

The astragalus sinicus is the beautiful result of labor pains
Between the plowed rows in the field
in the freezing cold winter.

Is this every strand a blade of dagger⋯
It would have been so before lifted its head.

When the sound of coming spring touches the rim of ears
It's blooming as a sedentary wild flower
I would cut it and design your fashionable clothes.

Blow the chapped hands puff, puff
And take it as warp yarn
Glittering crystal on the weft thread,
It's a love raised with tears.

When the warm spring sunshine shines
Your wounded heart will be comforted
By the red astragalus sinicus.

꽃과 나

꽃이
슬퍼지면 무엇이 되나요
가슴 아린 눈물 꽃 피우나요

꽃도 나도 슬픈데
우리는 어떡하나요

방울방울
눈물 뚝뚝 흘려야 하나요

너 때문이라고
옷소매 부여잡고 하소연하나요

쓰리도록 아파
서럽게 서럽게 울어야 하나요

꽃구름 되어
하염없이 흘러가야 하나요

아~
어쩌나요 어쩌나요.

Flower and Me

What will happen if a flower would be sad?
Heart breaking flower of tears would bloom···

Flower is sad and so do I,
So what shall we do!

Drop by drop
Should we shed tears···

Because of you
Shall I hold on your sleeves···
Complaining it's because of you.

The pain is so deep
Do I have to weep so sadly~

Becoming as a flower-like cloud,
Do I have to flow in the sky endlessly~

Oh~
I really don't know what to do.

꽃 청산 언덕에 올라

꽃이 좋아
꽃을 그렸습니다

바람이 좋아
바람을 노래했습니다

꽃바람
언덕에 올라
꽃이 되었습니다

그리고
눈을 감았습니다
꽃 나비들이
마구 날아다녔습니다

나는
꽃 같은 세월
꿈처럼 살았습니다

꿈같은 세월
꽃처럼 살았습니다.

On the Green Hill Covered with Flowers

I painted flowers
As I love flowers.

I sang to the wind
As I like the wind.

I climbed to the hill
Of spring breeze
And I became a flower.

There
I closed my eyes
The flower butterflies
Flew around here and there.

I lived
My flowery years
Like a dream.

My dreamy years
I lived like a flower.

꽃 피고 잎 지는 날

하늘히 피었다
하릴없이 지는 꽃이여

꽃 피는 날에 따라 웃고
꽃 지는 날엔 슬퍼 울어

잎 지는 날엔 푸른 눈물 떨구고
붉은 단풍 질 때 눈시울 붉혀라

오고 가는 계절에 웃고 울고
불고 가는 바람에 꽃 지고 잎 지고.

When Flowers Bloom and Leaves Fall

Beautifully bloomed
Flower, you fall without paying attention.

I laugh on the day when flower blooms
I cry sad on the day when the flower falls

I shed blue tears when the tree leaves fall,
I blush with tears when the red tree leaves fall

I laugh and weep when the season changes
In the blowing wind, flowers and tree leaves fall.

무심천에 바람 불면

무심천에 바람 불면
날마다 날마다 꽃이 피네

무심천에 청풍 불면
해마다 철 따라 꽃이 피네

꽃 피는 날은 따라 웃고
꽃 지는 날에 슬퍼 울어

잎 지는 날엔
푸른 눈물 떨구고

붉은 단풍 질 때
눈시울 붉히네

오고 가는 계절에
웃고 울고

불고 가는 바람에
꽃 피고 잎 지고.

가곡 2013- 박성균 곡, 홍승완 노래

When the Wind Blows in the River Mushimchon

When the wind blows in the River Musimchon,
Flowers bloom every day.

When the fresh wind blows in the River Mushimchon,
Flowers bloom every season every year.

I laugh in concert with the blooming flowers
I cry sadly when the flowers fall

On the day when the tree leaves fall
I shed tears of blue colors

When red tree leaves fall
I blush with tears

Upon changing seasons
I laugh or cry

In the blowing wind
Flower blooms and tree leaves fall.

Korean Gagok 2013— Composed by Park Sung Kyun,
Song by Hong Seung Wan

별들의 꿈

밤마다
저 많은 별이 반짝이는 건
잠 못 드는 사람들의
그리움 때문이다

하늘이 깊고 푸른 것은
도무지 알 수 없는 마음속

나는 너를 모르고
너는 나를 몰라
홀로 반짝이고 있는 것이다

아름다운 호숫가 숲속
풀숲에 내려앉을 날 그리며

꽃잎처럼 붉은 그리움
환영幻影 같이 피어날
그때를 꿈꾸며.

The Dream of the Stars

Every night
Countless stars are shining
Caused by the longing
Of the sleepless people.

Why the sky is so deep and blue
Is like the heart unable to guess.

As I don't know you
You don't know me either
It's shining alone.

Longing for the day when it settles down
In the beautiful lakeside forest.

The scarlet longing like petals
Dreaming of the time when it will
Bloom like an illusion.

숲속의 사계四季

별도 맑고
하늘도 맑고

봄이면
파르름 어여쁜
연둣빛 꿈속에 졸고

여름엔
무성한 숲 사이로 청랑한 물소리
삐삐새 호로록새 귀살쩍어

가을이면
서걱이는 낙엽 위에
구슬 밤 떨어지는 소리
다람쥐랑 마주 앉아 도토리 까기

겨울엔
폭폭 내려 쌓이는 눈 속에
노루 사슴처럼 뛰놀다가

발목 잡힌 개구리처럼
동안거冬安居에 들어
깊은 잠 자리라.

Four Seasons in the Forest

Stars are shining brightly
The sky is clear.

In the spring
Beautiful green lives
Doze in the light green dream.

In the summer
The sound of clean water through the lush forest
All the sounds of beeper bird, whistle bird tangled.

In autumn
The falling sound of bead-like chestnut
On the crisp falling leaves.
I shell the acorn sitting face to face with the squirrel.

In the winter
I will run like musk deer and deer
On the piling snow.

Like an ankle chained frog
I will have a deep sleep
In the shelter for the cold winter.

이 궁벽한 산기슭에

꽃 좋아하면 눈물 흔타고
꽃 좋아하면 외롭다고
그 누가 말했던가

떨어진 꽃잎 쓸어안고
아린 가슴 주체키 힘들어

외로움 깊어 병이 되어도
살구꽃 홀로 지는
무인 벽촌에

적막해 좋은 이 산골에
쓸쓸해 좋은 이 산촌에
살고 지고! 살고 지고!

청도라지꽃
머리에 꽂고 싸돌아다니다
산기슭 외진 곳에 누워 잘까

무덤가 들 귀퉁이 제비꽃처럼
사알짝 죽어져 고이 잠들까

아~ 이런 주책없는 심사…

At This Foothill

Someone said;
If she likes flowers, she will be full of tears
If she likes flowers, she will be lonely.

Embracing the fallen petals
I can't control my sore heart.

Even if the serious loneliness causes disease
In the uninhabited village
The apricot blossoms fall alone.

In this nice valley as it is serene
In this beautiful valley as it is lonesome.
I want to live and die here
Live and die here!

After wandering here and there
Decorating hair with blue broad bellflower
Shall I sleep in a lonely place at the foothill···

Shall I die unknowingly and fall asleep permanently
Like a violet at the corner of a grave···

Ah~ A wishy-washy thought!

잠자리, 그 아름다운 비상飛翔

하아얀 환희!
금은 사 쏟아지는 하늘

그물 빛 나래
까마득히 날리어

아스름~
푸르른 빛 속으로
저 무한의 공간으로

창공을 선회하는
무한대의 몸짓

한 쌍의 아름다운 비상.

Dragonfly, the Beautiful Flying

The white jubilance!
The gold and silver thread pour in the sky.

The transparent color wings
Fly at a long distance.

Far away
They fly into the blue light
Fly into that infinite space.

Infinite gesture
Of circling in the blue sky.

A pair of dragonflies' beautiful flying!

초원의 밤

그대여!
바람 불어 좋은 날
풀 내음 풀풀 날리는 초원으로 가자

초록 향기 번지는 언덕에 앉아
장진주사將進酒辭 한 가락에
솔가지에 걸린 상현달은
수묵 담채 송월도松月圖라

풍류 넘쳐 시흥을 돋우니
한세상 시름 중천에 뜬구름 같아라

사랑이여
꽃향기 번져오는 언덕으로 가자
가서, 풀벌레 소리 들으며
내려앉는 이슬에
옷자락 흠뻑 적시며 걸어보자

풀꽃들 지천에 깔린 초원의 푸른 밤
이 전원의 향기를 새벽이 오도록 마셔보자.

將進酒辭: 송강 정철의 사설시조 권주가
松月圖: 소나무와 달 그림

The Night in the Prairie

My dear!
Let's go to the prairie full of fluttering grass smells
On a beautiful windy day.

Sitting on the hill of green scent,
With the song of Jangjinjusa*
The moon that hangs on the pine branch
Is a scene of Songwoldo** painted with ink in light color!

The poetic mood overflows by the songs
The worry in the life is just like
A floating cloud in the middle of the sky.

My dear love,
Let's go to the hill where flower scent spreads
Go and hear the songs of grass bugs
On the dew
And walk in soaking dews at the skirt.

Blue nights of the prairie full of grasses and flowers
Let's inhale the fragrance of the prairie till
we meet the dawn.

* Jangjinjusa is a poetic song to invite wines.
  Poet Songgang Jungchul wrote the lyric.
** Songwoldo is a painting with pine and the moon

가을이 나를 두고

가을 산 깊은 골
선명히도 고운 가을빛 물든 나무들

몸도 마음도
한 폭의 수채화가 되어
단풍잎 쏟아지는 산자락에 앉아

내 시집 속 한 편의 시를
뉘 있어 듣든 말든…

시어들은
잡목 우거진 숲으로 날아들어
잎잎이 곱게 곱게 타올라
골골이 넘쳐흐르는 다홍 물결

때마침 불어오는 한 줄기 바람에
싱싱한 기억들 펄~펄 날리며
우수수 춤추는 가을 산

흩날려라!
격렬히 떨어지는 잎들이여
내 기억의 화폭에 담아두고 보리라

타거라!
왼 산이 탄다 한들 한 가슴만 할까

날아라!
활활 불꽃을 날려라

꽃불 되어 타올라라
혼불 되어 올라라

가는 길은
환희의 몸짓으로 갈지니.

Autumn Quits Me

In the deep valley in autumn
There are distinctly beautiful autumn colored trees.

My body and mind
Become a piece of watercolor
And sit on the foothill where maple leaves fall.

I recite one of my poems
Don't care anyone listens to it or not···

Poetic words
Fly into a bush lush forest
Every leaf burn finely.
A red wave overflows in every valley.

At this moment, the fresh wind blows
To remind me of the memories vividly
And the autumn hills rustling.

Fly high!
The wildly falling leaves
I will put them in the canvas of my memory
To see for a long time.

Burn as you will!
Even the whole hill burns,
it will be no bigger than my heart!

Fly high flame!
Burn up like a furious flame.

Burn up like a fire of the flower,
as a fire of my soul.

I will go my way
In a gesture of joyfulness.

갈대와 억새

강에서 우는 갈빛 울음
산에서 우는 흰빛 울음

갈빛 노래 조용히 흐르는 호숫가
산비탈엔 은빛 머리채 흩날리는 억새

바람 속의 갈대처럼
온몸으로 우는 그것이 삶이런가

바람 속의 억새처럼
흔들어 몸짓하는 것이 산다는 것인가

호수는 말없이
쓸쓸히 깊어만 가고.

The Reed and Silver Grass

The cry in the river is as brown as reed
The cry on the hill is white as silver grass.

Brown color song is sung along the lake shore
Silver grass silvery hair flutters on the hillside.

Is it a life crying with whole body
Like a reed in the wind⋯

Is it a life to live shaking a body
Like a silver grass in the wind⋯

The lake stays in solitude and silence
While the time moves deeper and deeper.

낙화落花

기쁨처럼 화사한
아리아리 고운 모습

하늘빛 바람에 실려
나르는 듯 가는 모습

받아줄 이 없는
연분홍 그 향으로
떨어져 내리는 꽃잎

울음 머금고
아릿다이 지는 꽃이여!

내 너를 위해
명인의 대금 소리를 들려주마

훌훌히 가는 너를 기려
이 땅의 숨결을 실어 보내마

가는 길도 고웁고
사라져도 고운 너를

어이어이 잊을 소냐

내 가슴에 지워지지 않는
화인花印을 남기고
가는 너를.

The Falling of Flowers

Beautiful appearance
As bright as joy.

On the wind in azure
The falling shape is like flying on the air.

The falling petals
With the fragrance of light pink
Nobody will take it though.

You, beautifully falling flower
With tears!

For you
I'll let you hear the sound of large bamboo flute
Played by a master.

In honor of you
Departing lonely.
I will let you carry the breathing of this earth.

Beautiful you, on your way so beautiful
Even though you may disappear.

How can I forget you!

Leaving you, falling flower
You left me a seal of flower
That can't be erased from my heart.

소리

지상엔 만 가지 꽃
하늘엔 헤아릴 수 없는 별
마음속엔 오만가지 생각

아아 ! 나는 어이 …

글로써 달래 볼거나
심상에 다가온 내 한 줄의 시가
허허로운 마음에 잠시 여운으로 남아

그 누구의 마음에 기쁨이 될까
그 누구의 가슴에 위로가 될까

하기야 내 앞가림도 부족하니
이 노릇 어이할꼬

그래도 당신의 가슴에
꽃 피고 잎 지는 소리
잎새에 스치는 바람 소리

자잘 자잘 여울물 소리
들리지 않나요.

The Sound

There are so many kinds of flowers on earth,
Countless stars in the sky,
And there is variety of thoughts in my head.

Ah! What shall I do···

Shall I soothe me by writing···
One line of my poem came to my thought
Stays a moment in my empty heart.

To whose mind will it be a joy···
To whose heart will it be a comfort···

Frankly, I'm not a person to look after myself.
I don't know what to do.

However, don't you hear them in your heart;
The sound of blooming flower, falling leaves
The sound of the wind blowing on the leaves

The sound of gently flowing water in the stream.

유년의 고향

노오란 들판 위에 새파란 하늘
새털구름 뭉게구름 그린 듯 고웁고
팔랑팔랑 손짓하는 미루나무

싸릿가지 끝에 앉았던 고추잠자리
쨍한 볕살 타고 나르는 빨간 꼬리
따라 잡겠다고 내닫던 날들

무명 옷감 하얗게 펼쳐진 들길에
그리움이 깔린다

논둑길 따라 사뭇 내달리면
시원스런 개울물 소리
바윗돌 자갈돌 뒤집으며
첨벙첨벙 자잘 대던 아이들

그리운 벗들이여!
메뚜기 톡톡 뛰던 들판
벼 숲을 헤치며 너도 뛰고 나도 뛰고

강아지풀에 다닥다닥 꿰어
노을이 내려앉은 어스름 길
통치마 자락 적시며
돌아오는 이슬 젖은 들녘

잠자리 나래 사이로 비치는
투명 그물 빛 하늘이 그리워
용수철처럼 튀어 오르는 추억들

웬일인가요
가는 세월에도 뜬금없이 내닫는
내 유년의 달음박질.

Hometown in My Childhood

The blue sky above the yellow field
It's so beautiful like a painting of cirrus clouds
and fleecy clouds
And the eastern poplar that makes a dancing gesture.

Red dragonfly used to sit on the edge of bush clover.
The days when I ran to catch it following its red tail
flying in the bright sunshine.

My longing expands
On the agricultural road in the field
the where white cotton cloth spreads.

When I ran fast along the bank of rice paddies
I could hear the sound of cool water running in the brook.

We were the children who chirped
While flipping the rocks and pebbles.

My good old friends!
The field where the grasshoppers jump
You and I used to run through the rice fields.

Chained in clusters on the green foxtail
On the sunset twilight road in the evening
We returned home from the field wet by dew
While our seamless one-piece skirts were also wet.

Our memories sprang up like a spring
As we missed the transparent blue sky
That was shined through the wing of dragonflies.

What happened?
The running into my child days out of nowhere
Even though the years have passed.

파도

파도여!
까마득한 날, 하늘이 열리던
그날에 이 땅을 보았더냐

파도여!
그 언제부터 해변을 연모했더냐

그토록 한결같은 간절한 몸짓으로
하얀 바람 물결 넘실대는 출렁임으로

물안개 흩날리며 달려와
부서지도록 휘감아 네 사랑을 노래했더냐

쏴아~~
밤새 애원하듯 들려오는 절절한 소리는
어느 태곳적 소리이더냐

별 헤이고 별 지는 밤
달빛도 물이 되어 흐르고

파도 너는 왜
가슴팍에 파고들어 나를 적시느냐.

The Wave

You, wave!
Did you see this earth on the day
When the sky was opened long, long time ago···

You wave!
Since when have you loved the beach···

In such a steady, passionate gesture
With fluctuating white ripples of the wind.

You came running scattering the milky fog,
You sang your love winding up even to break yourself!

The sound of high sea~~
What kind of old age sound is this
That I hear as if it begs all night long···

The stars are counted and setting in the night
The moonlight also flows like water.

Why are you, wave,
Penetrating into my chest and making me wet with tears?

홀로 지는 꽃

쓸쓸한 저녁
호젓이 피었다
외로이 지는 꽃

햇살도 흩어져 내리고
알 길 없는 여윈 마음
하~ 스산해

무엇이 있는가
밤과 낮, 이 공간에
아무것도 없다

바보 같은 내가 있을 뿐
한 송이 도라지꽃처럼
파랗게 멍든 내가

너는 어이
나를 이리도 상심케 하느냐

제 슬픔 제 설움에
홀로 지는 꽃이여.

The Flower Falling Alone

One lonesome evening,
The flower blooms quietly
And falls lonely.

The sun shines with scattered rays
The damaged heart that I can't understand
So dreary and lonesome!

What exists
In the space between night and day?
There's nothing!

There's only a stupid one like me
I've been bruised blue
Like a balloon flower

How come
You hurt me so seriously?

In my sadness
You, the flower that falls alone
At your own sorrow!

공허空虛

산사에 풍경소리 없다면
이 정적靜寂을 어찌할꼬

해변에 파도 소리 없다면
저 황량함을…

들판에 바람이 없다면
그 허허로움을 어이할꼬

태초에 말씀이 있었느니라
또한 적막함이 있었노라

그리하여
내 가슴에 치유되지 않는
막막한 아픔이 자리 하노라.

The Vanity

If there's no sound of temple bell
How should I overcome the silence!

If I can't hear the waves on the beach
How can I calm my desperation!

If there is no wind in the field
What can I do for my futile heart!

In the beginning there were the Words.
There was also the silence.

Therefore
There is an incurable serious pain in my heart;
The vanity.

바다, 그 태고太古의 소리

저 바닷가에 누워
파도 소리를 들어라

사념思念도 허물도 벗어놓고
몸도 마음도 놓아버리고
한바탕 생의 꿈도 떨쳐버리고

그저 그렇게
바다와 같이 숨 쉬어라

와락 달려와 안기는 파도
와르르 쏟아지는 물안개
두 팔 가득 안았다 놓았다

하얗게 부서지는 물거품
심장 깊숙이 마셨다 뿜었다

안길 때는 간절함으로
떠날 때는 애틋함으로
나를 쓰다듬어라

바다
그 드넓은 가슴에 드러누워
뜨는 해 품었다

석양엔 지는 해로 내어주리

까만 하늘에 뜨는 별은
내 가슴에 푸른 별

보랏빛 새벽 오면
파도에 실려 보내리라

밀물 썰물
들고 나는 쉼 없는 파도소리
영겁永劫 속으로 억만 겁이 지났으련만

천지간에 미물微物
인간은 그대의 그리움

지상인지 천상인지
이 세상에서
가장 아득한 소리

까마득히 들릴 듯 말 듯
사라질 때까지

유한有限의 존재여 !
무한無限의 소리를 들어라

그 太古의 소리를…

The Sea, the Sound of Ancient Times

Lay down on the beach
Listen to the sound of the waves.

Apart from your thoughts and faults
Get off your body and your mind
Even forgetting the greatest dream in your life.

In such a way
Breathe as the sea does.

The wave rushes toward you and hugs
The water mist will be poured en mass
Repeatedly hugging it all up
White scattering water foam
Repeatedly breathing deeply into the heart.

Caress me
Earnestly when hugging,
Affectionately when leaving.

The sea
Lie down on your wide breast
I embraced the rising sun
At sunset, I will let it be a setting sun.

The rising star in the black sky
Is the blue star in my heart.

When the purple dawn comes
I will let myself be carried by the waves.

Rising tide and ebbing
The sound of the waves coming and going
Millions of millions of years would have passed into eternity

The creature of no account on earth and heaven,
Man is your longing.

Whether on the earth or in heaven
The remotest sound in this world
Is hardly heard from the distance
Till it disappears.

The limited existence of life,
Listen to the sound of infinity.

The sound of the ancient times.

바람의 노래

오늘도 나는
머리카락 흩날리는 바람 속에 서서
그대의 노래를 듣노라

바람은
포플러 잎에 반짝이는 손짓으로
가닥가닥 흩어지는 솔향기로
열리고 싶은 꽃망울 어루고파

바람은
나뭇가지 무성한 잎들의 수런거림으로
갈대꽃 하얀 넋 춤추는 머리채로
억새꽃 억센 바람을 그리워함에
폴폴 연분홍 꽃잎 날리고파

바람은
푸르름 성성한 숲의 일렁임으로
서걱이는 갈잎 소리
쌍골죽 젓대 소리로

바람은
할미꽃 솜털의 포근함으로
들꽃 애잔한 모습으로
꽃향기 뿜어나는 취객으로
한 잎 장미 꽃잎의 감미로운 미소로

출렁이는 물결 춤추는 파도로
오늘도 바람은 노래한다

모든 생명들의 생생한 기쁨을 위하여
바람의 변신은 무죄.

The Song of the Wind

Today as usual,
I hear your song standing in the wind
While my hair is dancing in the air.

The wind
Wishes to achieve the desire of the flower bud to open,
With glittering hand gestures on the poplar leaves
At the fragrance of pine scattering strand by strand.

The wind
Longs for the gust wind of silver grass flower
With dancing hair in the white soul of reed flower
With the whispering of lush leaves
It wishes to make the pink petals fly in the air.

The wind is
In the swaying of the lush green forest
The rustling sound of the reed leaves
With the sound of ssanggol bamboo flute*

The wind

With the warmth of the fine hairs of pasqueflower,

In the appearance of childish wild flowers

As a drunken person scented with the flower

With the sweet smile of a piece of rose petal.

The wind sings today as usual

As a rushing flow, as a dancing wave.

The wind sings today

For the cheerful joy of all lives

Transformation of the wind is not guilty!

* ssanggol bamboo flute – two sides wave bamboo flute

사랑을!

꽃향기 새소리
못 견디게 아름다운 날

감성 앞에 이성이 외로울 때
이성 앞에 감성이 눈물겨울 때

스산한 바람 소리 옷깃 스치우는
올 것 같지 않던 세월

봄 여름
내게도 그런 시절 있었던가
꽃그늘 아래 붉도록 서 있는 이여

나뭇잎마다 단풍 들어 고운 날
그 누가 사랑을 모를까

청춘!
당신에게도 쓸쓸한 날 오거든
빈 주머니에 낙엽 하나 넣고
산자락 들길을 걸어보라

먼 훗날
당신이 꽃이었나 잎이었나.

Love is!

One unbearably beautiful day
With the scent of flowers and songs of the birds,

When reason is lonely in front of emotion
When emotion is tearful in front of reason

The years when the sound of chilly wind brushing my
clothes
seemed to never come.

Spring and summer did I have such time!
You, who are standing under the shadow of the flower
until your face becomes red.

On the fine day when every leaf becomes autumn leaf,
who will not feel love!

Youth!
If you face a scary day,
put a piece of leaf in your pocket
And walk along the mountain trail.

In the remote future
Will you think you were a flower or a leaf···

자작나무 숲속에서

바람 부는 날엔
흰빛 서늘한
자작 나무 숲으로 가라

펄럭이는 바람에 슬픈 그
기다림처럼
자작이며 서 있는 숲으로 가라

고독도 쓸쓸함도
자작나무 숲속에 흩어버리고

흰 치마 속적삼으로
달빛 흠뻑 적시며
훨훨 정신없이 쏘다녀라

까무러치게 지치면
슬픔처럼
희슴프레 껑충히 서 있는

그 하얀 숨결에
몸을 통째로 맡기고 기대어보라

가슴속 시린 핏줄이
네 심장에 전율하리라

백화피白樺皮 벗는 소리 …
바람에 타는 향기

은회색 바삭이는 화촉향樺燭香.

In the Birch Forest

On a windy day
Go to the birch forest
In white color and feel cool.

Go to the forest
Where they stand whispering
Like the sorrowful waiting
At the fluttering winds.

Scatter the solitude and loneliness
In the birch forest.
Wander as much as you wish
Making the white skirt and underwear

Soaked by the moonlight.

If you get tired losing your sense,
You will stand with lost sense in faint appearance
Like sorrow

Let your whole body lean
On the white one's breathing.

The sore blood lines in your heart
Would give thrill to you.

The sound of peeling off the birch tree's white skin.
Smell of burning in the wind.

Incense of the newly married silvery gray bustling.

차 한 잔을 마시며

생각했습니다
무엇을 쓸까 무엇을 그릴까 하고

지난봄 가경 골 빛 고운 살구 꽃차
감나무골 산책길의 단풍잎 차

기억하기 싫은 일은
찻잔에 오르는 수증기로 날리고

기분 좋은 차 한 잔에
시상詩想은 어디론가 달아나고

오늘도 다가올 내일도
무언가 속삭임이 들리는듯합니다

마시고 또 마시고
지난 추억들을 채워 마셨지요

밤하늘에 반짝이는 별처럼
풀꽃들이 살며시 일러 주네요

한 줄의 시가
아름다운 언어의 모태임을…

Drinking a Cup of Tea

I thought many times
What to write and what to draw.

Those are the nice looking apricot blossom tea
in the Gagyung village last spring
And the maple leaf tea in the Gamnamugol village
on my promenade.

The things that I don't want to remember
I blow up with vapors rising over the cup.

With a fine mood of a cup of tea
The idea for a poem disappears somewhere.

It seems that I hear something whispering to me
For today and the days to come.

I drink a cup of tea
I filled up my past memories in the cup.

Like a twinkling star in the night sky
Grass flowers remind me confidentially.

That a line of a poem
Is the birthplace of beautiful language…

흔적痕迹

선택 불허의 자취
좋건 싫건
원하든 아니든

점이든 선이든
현재 이 시대를 살고 간 흔적

한때, 나는
자취 없이 사라지는 걸
인생의 큰
좌우명처럼 생각하며 살았다

잎새에 살랑이는 바람처럼
하롱하롱
꽃잎처럼 지고 싶다고

화사한 햇살 속으로
내 왔었다는 기억조차 없이
어디론가 사라지고 싶었다

그러나 지금 나는
내 뜻이든 아니든

시인詩人이라 불리우는
내 작은 삶의 흔적

지울래야 지울 수 없는
시詩라는 이 필적筆跡을.

The Trace

The trace of no choice
Whether I like it or not
Whether I wish it or not.

The trace of living in this age
Whether it is a dot or a line.

Once, I
Used to live thinking that
Disappearing without a trace
Is a big motto of my life.

I wished to pass away like a petal does
Halong halong~
Rashly like a breeze on a leaf.

I wanted to disappear somewhere
In the bright sunshine
Without even remembering that I came here.

However, I am now
Whether it is my will or not

The trace of my little life is
Called a poet

I can't erase the trace of poems
That I have ever made though I try.

Kwon Oh-jeong

poet song writer
Pen Name: Wunyoung 雲影
Born in Chunyang Bongwha Kyungbuk-do
E-mail: koj8835@hanmail.net
HP: 010-6567-8835(in Korea)
      +82-10-6567-8835(outside of Korea)
Daum Blog: 꽃 청산 언덕에 올라(in Korean)

Member of
International PEN Korea Center, The
  Korea Writers Association, Poetry
  Association, Modern Poets Association
  and Song Writers Association

Songs
사랑은 그대에게 Love for my dear
오월이 오면 When May comes
참꽃 피어 서럽네 I'm sad in the season of the
  azaleas
파도여! Oh, the wave
꽃 청산 언덕에 올라 On the hill covered with
  flowers
한생년 살고지고 May live long
만파식적 The flute to calm down tens of
  thousand waves

Published books
1st collection of poetry
  『꽃불 The Fire of Flowers』
2nd collection of poetry
  『황금 실타래 Golden Thread Roll』
3rd collection of poetry
  『백년의 미소 The Smile since Hundred
  Years』
4th collection of poetry
  『꽃 청산 언덕에 올라 On the Hill Covered
  with Flowers』
5th collection of poetry
  『무심천에 바람 불면 When the Wind
  Blows in the River Mushimchon』

6th collection of poetry
  『꽃이여! 바람이여! Oh, Flowers, Winds』
7th collection of poetry Korean-English
  『꽃과 바람의 노래 The Song of the
  Flowers and Winds』

Electronic books
『꽃불 The Fire of Flowers』
『황금 실타래 Golden Thread Roll』
『백년의 미소 The Smile for Hundred Years』
『꽃 청산 언덕에 올라 On the Hill Covered
  with Flowers』

Awards
Jikji Award Chooungju City 청주시직지상
  Collection of poetry 詩集『꽃 청산 언덕에
  올라 On the Hill Covered with Flowers』
1st Grand Prix Maehun Munhak 매헌문학
  상대상 Poem 詩〈思無邪花 Right Mind
  Flower〉
5th Yeonam Munhak Art award 제5회 연암
  문학예술상 Collection of poems 詩集『무
  심천에 바람 불면 When the Wind Blows
  in the River Musimchon』
12th Noh Chun-myung Literature Award
  노천명문학상 Collection of poems 詩集
  『꽃이여! 바람이여! Oh, Flowers, Wind』
The Nationwide Academy Fine Art Grand
  Exhibition 전국아카데미미술대전
Dong-Ah International Fine Art Grand
  Exhibition 동아국제미술대전
Baekje Grand Calligraphy Exhibition 백제서
  예대전수상

2부

번역: 권오정

2nd Part
Translated by
Kwon Oh−jeong

천상별곡天上別曲

태초에 천지를 창조하다

천지가 혼돈하고 공허함에 빛이 있으라!
빛과 어둠을 나누어 낮과 밤이라 칭하노라

궁창을 하늘이라 칭하고
천하의 물이 한곳에 모여 바다이고
뭍을 땅이라 칭하노라

땅에는 풀과 씨 맺는 채소
열매 맺는 나무와
움직이는 모든 생물을 내노라

인간은 내 형상대로 남과 여를 만드노니
생육하고 번성하여 땅에 충만 하라

고기 떼 춤추는 바다
새들과 바람이 떠다니는 하늘
만학천봉이 모두 그대의 것이니

모든 자연과 생물을 잘 다스리어
세세토록 복스런 삶을 누릴 지어다.

Heavenly Song

Create heaven and earth in the beginning

The sky and the earth are chaotic and
the light is emptiness!
We divide light and darkness and call it day and night.

That wide space is called the sky
The waters of the world are gathered in one place,
and becomes the sea
The hills and mountains are called the land

On the ground are grass and seed-bearing vegetables
The fruit-bearing tree
Give out all the living things that move

Human makes men and women in my form.
Grow and multiply and fill the earth.

A sea of fishs dancing
The sky with birds and the wind
All the mountain peaks are yours.

You have a good command of all nature
and living creatures
live a life of eternal happiness.

봄이 오는 소리

사르륵 사르르 꽃눈이 내려요
소르륵 소르르 봄비가 내려요

대지의 살갗 밑에 잠자던 새싹들
쏘오옥 쏙 기지개 켜는 소리

몽올몽올 꽃망울 맺는 소리
봉글봉글 꽃잎 벙그는 소리

꽃 나비 팔랑팔랑
날개짓 소리

저만큼 들녘에
아른아른 아지랑이 소리

님이여! 사랑이여 !
미소를 뿌리세요

사무치게 아리따운
황홀한 봄을 위하여.

The Sound of Spring is Coming

The sarreuk Sarre flower buds fall.
The Sorreuk Sorres Spring Rain falls.

The buds that had been asleep
under the skin of the earth.
The sound of a cow stretching

The sound of the blooming
The bubbling of the petals

Flower butterfly palang palang
a winging sound

In the field as far as it is
Shimmer of air

My dear! My love!
Spread smile with a smile

astoundingly beautiful
For the spellbound spring.

꽃불

불이 났습니다
산천에 불이 났습니다

심심산골 모롱이 모롱이
천지 강산에 불이 났습니다

산수유 개나리
노란 옷 입히던 봄볕
따끈따끈 쌓이더니

이내 만산홍화萬山紅花의
붉은 불이 붙었습니다

진달래 가지마다 횃불 밝혀
봄 속을 헤치며 마구 타오릅니다

봄은 꽃불 속에 숨어
활활 타고 있습니다

꽃들은
아지랑이 되어 하늘하늘
나비처럼 날아갑니다.

Flower Fire

There's a fire!
The mountain stream is on fire

Deep mountains, here and there
The mountains of heaven and earth are on fire

Cornelian cherry and forsythia
the yellow drapery of the spring sun
It was warm and warm

In the mountains in one moment
The red light is on

Azalea branches light a torch
Through the spring The fire burns

Spring hides in the flower fire
It's blowing a spark.

The flowers
Hannell hannell~ like haze
It flies like a butterfly.

복사꽃 흩날리면

복사꽃이 ~
복사꽃이 흩날리면

나도 같이
희희낙락 떨어지리라

꽃따라 물 따라
저 강가로 가리라

낙화 되어 흐르리라

꽃잎처럼 ~~
꽃잎처럼 떠가리라.

Peach Blossoming

Peach flowers
When the peach blossoms fly,

I'm like a petal
I shall laugh and fall.

Along the flowers with water
Go over to the river

It will flow like a fallen flower

Like petals~~
I'll float like that petals.

나 가고 나면

슬퍼하지 말아요
아주 잠깐만 기억해요

아슴푸레한 추억처럼

그리곤
잊어요
꽃을 잊듯이
잊어요

옛날 그 옛날처럼
잊어버려요

사라진 구름처럼
영 ~ 영 잊어요

스쳐 간 옷깃처럼
불고 간 바람처럼.

When I'm Gone

Don't be sad.
Just remember for a minute

Like a distant memory

And then···
Forget it.
Forget the flowers
Forget it.

Like the old days
Forget it.

Like a cloud has disappeared
Forget it forever.

Like a passing dress
Like a gust of wind.

한 송이 꽃처럼

고운 사람 앞에선
고운 사람으로

아름다운 사람 앞에선
아름다운 사람으로

그네의 맘속에 들어
고운 이로 살고파

오가는 길목 한적한 터에
꽃 심고 나무 심어

연분홍 아련한
한 송이 꽃처럼
고운 사람으로 살고 싶어.

Like a Flower

In front of a fine man
with a fine person

In front of a beautiful person
with a beautiful person

In his heart
I want to live as a nice woman

On the way, in a quiet place
Planting flowers and planting trees

Pinkish-tinted
like a flower
I want to live as a nice person.

그림과 시

그 누가
그림은 소리 없는 시요
시는
형상 없는 그림이라 했지요

그림은 무언가 그리워서 그리고
그리움은 텅~빈 마음

시가 있는 그림, 그림이 있는 시

시란 언어의 예술
아름답고 행복한 순간의
소박한 심상을 그린 것

한 줄의 시가
우리를 맑고 깊게 합니다

사랑하는 사람들을 위하여
최선의 성실한 하루를 위하여
진실한 삶을 위하여

영혼을 건드리는 여운
시詩, 그 아름다운 언어를 위하여.

Pictures and Poetry

A man of the name
The picture is silent poetry
The poem
It was called a picture without shape.

A picture of something in the longing
Nostalgia is an empty heart

A picture of poetry
A poem with a picture

Art of poetry language
Beautiful and happy moments
a simple imagery

A phrase from a poetry
It makes us clear and deep

For the love of the people
For the best and most sincere day
For a true life

A soulful touch
Poems, for their beautiful language.

네 피를 마시며

네 피를 탐하여
너를 들이킨다

꽃잎 나뭇잎 피우려
겨우내 간직한 너의 지기地氣를

아! 달콤 싱그런 내음이여
Dracula의 희열에 취해~~

속죄의 날은 언제 일러냐
지상에서 영원으로~

하여,
그대 몸속 수액으로 회귀하리.

Drinking your Blood

In a covetous interest in your blood
I inhale you

To make petals and leaves bloom.
You have the energy of your land

Oh! Sweet and fresh.
Dracula's joy~~

When is the day of atonement?
From the ground to the eternity

Therefore
I will return to your body sap.

시인을 위하여

가을엔
당신의 창가에 귀뚜리가 되겠습니다
쓸쓸하고 서글픈 사람들에게 전해주세요
밤새도록 울어대는 놈 있다고

겨울이면
당신의 창에 흰 눈으로 내리겠습니다
서러운 이에게 전해주세요
서리서리 쌓인 한
흩날리는 축복이 되었노라고

여름날엔
한 쌍의 잠자리로 날겠습니다
사랑을 찾는 이에게 전해주세요
그토록 절묘한 비상

그물 빛 나래에 부서지는
하늘빛을 보라고

봄 그날엔
노랑나비로 오겠습니다
대지에 피어나는
풀꽃들의 황홀함을 위하여

푸른 꿈 간직한 이들에게 전해주세요
이 세상엔 아직도
가슴 벅찬 일들이 많고 많다고

시인이여! 그대
촉촉하고 애틋한 마음
그들의 가슴에
한 송이 들꽃을 심어주세요.

For the Poet

In autumn
I'll be a cricket by your window
Tell the lonely and sad people
There's a guy crying all night.

In winter
I'll come down to your window
with a white snow
Please tell the sad people
As long as it's frosty
It's a blessing to scatter.

On a summer day
I'll fly in a pair of dragonflys.
Tell the person who seeks love
Such an exquisite winging

The broken wings of a light net
Look at the sky

On spring day
I'll be back in the yellow butterfly.
Blooming on earth
For the ecstasy of grass and flowers

Tell the blue dreamers hidden it.
Still in this world
There's a lot of heartbreaking stuff.

Poet! You
Moist and tender heart
In their hearts
Plant a wild flower.

고엽枯葉

깊어가는 가을
지난 기억들 추억으로 날리고

나뭇잎은 쓰르르 떨어져
공원의 비인 의자에
포도 위에 내려앉아
스산한 발길들을 머무르게 하고

하늘 환한 나뭇가지
마지막 남은 잎새들
그 빛
그 모습 그지없이 고웁다

갈바람은
떠난다고 하소연하는데
철없는 웃음소리
까르르 은행잎은 쏟아지고

건반에 구르는 고엽 소리와 함께
내 그리움, 아쉬움 몰라라
쓸쓸히 저물어가는 가을.

The Fallen leaves

A deep autumn
I'm gonna blow it up with memories

The leaves fall apart in a park chair
on the street
And let them stay on their lonely feet.

Branches with bright sky
The last remaining leaves
The light
I am so glad to see it

Autumn wind
I'm complaining about leaving.
A bleak laugh
Carre, the ginkgo leaves are pouring,

With the sound of the old leaves rolling
on the keys
I don't know my longing, my regret
Fall, falling to the ground.

꽃차 한 잔의 추억

지난 가을 가경천 산책길
노랑 빨강 빛 고운 단풍잎

차 숟갈에 꽃잎 하나
다호엔 매화 한 송이
흑단 목 다반에 차려놓고

기쁜 일 슬픈 일 꿀 한 스픈
따끈한 차 한 잔에

지난 추억 모락모락 피어나는
그윽한~
꽃차 한 잔의 향기.

Memories of a Cup of FlowersTea

Last fall, a promenade along the stream of
Gagyeong-river side
yellow red and light maple leaves

The one petal teaspoon
A plum blossoms in a tea jar
A memorial table and
it's just one of ebony wood

A happy thing, a sad thing, a sugar slug
In a cup of hot tea

Boiled up past memories to bloom
The fragrant~
Flower scent of a cup of tea.

황홀한 침묵

그대 앞에
나는 한 송이 꽃

명주실 실바람으로
나를 어루소서

명주 천
보드라운 손수건으로
어루소서

잎새에 머무는
연둣빛 손짓은
애잔한 실눈으로 맞으리

꽃몽오리 분홍빛 애무는
곱디고운 눈길로 반기리

그대 감미로움에
꽃잎 하나 파르르 떨었습니다

아리아리 고운 자태
꽃무리 속에 숨었습니다.

A Ecstatic Silence

Before you
I'm a flower

With a fine wind of silk
Touch me.

Silk thread
A soft handkerchief
Take care of yourself

In the leaves
A light green gesture
with a gentle look

The pink-colored petting
Of the flower bud with a fine eye

In your sweetness
One petal, was trembling

Ari ari fine figure
I hid in a bunch of flowers.

3부

3rd Part

Poems published
on various
literary magazines

봄과 나비

봄님!
새뜻새뜻 풀 옷 단장하셨나요
산들산들 바람 타고 날으리이까

봄님!
제비꽃 할미꽃 피우셨나요
애틋한 마음으로 살피올까요

봄님!
산에 산에 진달래
붉은 마음 활짝 피우셨나요
훨~ 훨~ 춤 한마당 벌리올까요

봄님!
보랏빛 라일락 안개구름처럼
그 향기 어지러운가요

봄 나비
향 묻은 나래로
님의 옷에 옮으올까요

님 눈썹의 그림자
꽃잎 손수건으로 닦으올까요.

Spring and Butterflies

Spring!
Did you freshen up your new clothes?
Let's go in the wind and fly.

Spring!
Did you bloom violets and Pasque(halmi) flowers?
I'll take care of you with a pity.

Spring!
Azaleas on mountains
You're all red in your heart.
I'm gonna dance a lot more.

Spring!
Like a purple lilac cloud of fog.
Is that smelly?

Spring butterfly
With fragrant wings
I'll move it to your clothes.

Shadow of the nim eyebrow
I'll wipe it with a petal handkerchief.

쪽빛 바다

봄 바다가 하늘을 만나면
하늘빛이 된다

하늘도 바다를 만나면
물빛이 된다

바다에서도 하늘 아래서도
내가 먼저 파랗게 물이 든다

허허로운 영혼의 빈 공간
그저 멍하니

하늘가 아득한 수평선을 바라보며
망연한 설레임의 비상을 꿈꾼다

남빛 출렁이는 바닷가에서.

PEN2017 세계한글작가대회기념시집-한영대표작

Indigo Sea

When the spring sea meets the sky
It turns into the blue sky

When the sky meets the seaIt turns into water

Even in the sea
Beneath the sky
First of all, I drink blue

Empty Space of the Soul of the
In a fool's ear

Beyond the Sky
Look at the distant horizon
Dream of flying

On the
shores of the sea
Blue waves on the beach.

Translated by the author
The 3rd World Korean Writers' Competition 2017

참꽃 피어 서럽네

적막 산천
참꽃 피어 서럽네

무덤가에 제비꽃
무덤 위에 할미꽃

지천 산천
참꽃 피어 서럽네

꽃을 희롱하는 흰나비
눈가에 어지러워

하늘하늘～～
꽃나비 어지러워
하롱하롱～～
꽃나비 어지러워

내 가슴에 온통
참꽃 피어 서럽네

참꽃 피어 서럽네.

가곡 정덕기 곡, 서활란 노래-2018

Azaleas are Sad When they bloom

Desolate mountain stream
I'm sad to see the azalea bloom.

Violets on the grave
Halmi flower above the grave

In the mountains and in the field
I'm sad to see the azalea blossoms.

A white butterfly that teases flowers
I'm dizzy in the before of my eyes

A flake a flake~~
Flower Butterfly dizzy
Halong harong~~
Flower Butterfly dizzy

All over my chest
I'm sick of Azalea blossoms

I'm sad to see the azalea blossom.

Composed by Chung Duk–Ki, Song by Suh Hwal–Ran 2018

오월이 오면

연둣빛 짙어 오는 봄날
실안개 아른거리는
깨끼저고리 갑사 치마 차려입고

수틀에 모여드는 나비처럼
꽃향기 흩날리는 들판으로
봄맞이 가리라

인조견 흰 속치마
풀물이 들도록
금잔디 강변을 줄달음쳐 보리라

내 가슴에 흠뻑, 봄물이 들면

유유히 흐르는 저 강물 따라
녹음방초 지천에 깔린
꽃 청산 유람 떠나리라.

poetry Korea 2017— 6호

When May comes

On a spring day when a green light is densing,
A haze of mist glimmer and waver
I will dress up in a coat and a "Gapsa" skirt.

Like butterflies over the embroidery frame,
Flowering fragrance on the field
I will feel spring.

The white silk skirt
To gets dyed with grass,
I will run along the river with green grass.

In the bosom of my heart,
When it becomes full with the feeling of spring,

Along the flowing stream of the river
Full of grass and flowers
It will leave for the flower of the blue mountain.
I will go sightseeing.

poetry Korea 2017—No.6

꿈길

재 넘어 고개 넘어 하얀 길
무작정 가고 싶은
꿈속처럼 그리운 길

산등성이
붉은 소나무처럼 휘어진 길
누군가 손짓하는 고갯마루 산마루

옷자락 꿈자락 날리며
꿈길 같은 길을 따라
날마다 날마다 길을 나선다

꿈결 속에 꿈길
길 따라 나서면
내 그리움 있을까

저 길 따라나서면
내 그리움 잠잘까.

poetry Korea 2018-7호

Dream Way

The white road beyond over the hill
Where I want to go mindlessly
a path as long as it is in a dream
the way I miss in my dreams

mountain ridge
A curved path like a red pine tree
A hillside ridge where someone beckons

Dreaming of the skirt
Along the path of dreaming
I go on my way every day

Dream to unite in dream
Along the way
I miss you

If you follow that path
My longing sleep

poetry Korea 2018—No.7

오늘이 내 마지막 날이라면

나는 이 하루를
내 작은 정원에 나가
풀꽃을 심으리라

싸리 꽃대 하나 찾아 심으리라
먼 훗날 누군가
홍 보랏빛 고운 모습 애틋해 올리라

뽀오얀 안개 자우룩한 날
모든 아름다움이 내 가슴에 녹아들어
세상 하직하기 아주 썩 좋은 날

자연을 노래하는
시인만 남은 여기

나 홀로 쓸쓸한 봄날에 사라지리라
아지랑이 되어 하롱하롱 사라지리라.

제4회 세계한글작가대회 영문대표작선집 2018.11

If today is my last day

I have this day
Get out in my little garden
Plant a flower.

I'll find a sack of flowers and plant it.
Some day later someone
It looks like a pinkish red.

A day with a foggy mist
All the beauty melts in my heart
It's a very good day to get out of the world

Singing nature
Only poets left here

I'll be gone alone on a lonely spring day
I will become a haze and disappear.

The Collection of Poetry & Prose in English to Celebrate the 4th 2018. 11

엄마의 숲

동구 밖 유년의 동산
꿈속에 내 어머니 날 안아 올리시던 곳

부러운 눈길 몰라라 댕기머리 처녀들
긴 동아줄 잡고 그네 타던 곳

들 가운데 당산나무 숲속
멋들어진 연리목 소나무

이토록 늠름한 기상으로 튼실하게 지켜주심을
예전엔 미처 몰랐지요

세월 훌쩍 흐른 이제사 어머님 여기에 계신 걸
무명 앞치마 자락 애끓는 정 어이 두고 가셨는지

메뚜기 뛰놀던 황금벌판
봄 냇가 버들피리 불던 곳

떠나도 다시 또 가는 기약 없는 유년의 그리움
마음 한 잎 거둘 곳 없는 허망한 놀이터로 떠납니다.

한국문인협회 – '나의 고향 나의 어머니' 2019

My Mother's Forest

On a little hill of my youth at the outskirts of a village
my mother used to raise me up in her arms

Where young maidens with the ribbons on their hair
used to enjoy on a swing indifferently to the envious eyes

Two great pine trees has become one in natural graft
in the middle of a field where a tree shrine stands

I didn't know how supportive you were
with vigorous spirit protecting us by then

After so many years have passed, I now realize
you are here with all your motherly affection left behind

In the golden field where locusts were jumping around
by the stream I used to play a willow pipe in spring

Longing for the youth long gone in time takes me in vain
to the playground that can't take a piece of my mind

The Korean Writers Association —'My Mother in My Hometown' 2019

바람아!

오늘도 바람이 분다
나의 친구 바람아

네가 서성이고 있는 빈들
네가 거닐고 있는 뜨락

어제도 그제도
내 오랜 친구 바람아
지금 나는 너를 노래한다

네 쓸쓸함
네 황량함
네 스산한 발자국을

언제나 내게는
너 바람뿐이란 걸
나는 알기 때문이다

나의 사랑 바람아!

Poetry Korea 8호-2019

Wind!

The wind blows today
My friend's amigo

The empty ones you're walking around
The heat you're walking around

Yesterday and the day before yesterday
My old friend, the Wind
Now I sing you

your loneliness
your desolation
Your tired footprints

Always for me
You're the only one with the wind.
Because I know

My love, my wind!

Poetry Korea No.8—2019

홀홀히 가오신 님아

님아!
호올로 가오신 님아
나만 홀로 외오 두고
홀홀히 가오신 님아

님은 갔습니다
푸른 물 파도 길로
철렁철렁 떨치고 갔습니다

떠오르는 빛으로 왔다가
석양에 그림자 드리우며
노을빛 이랑 길을
성성히 밟으며 갔습니다

화목火木이 되겠다던
스스로의 다짐은 어이 두고
홀홀히 가셨나요

아아! 님은 갔지만
님의 글은 남아있습니다

바다를 산천을
그 발길 간데 족족
시어로 노래로
남겨놓고 가시었습니다.

한국시인 대표작– 사랑시집

The lonely gone, My dear

Oh! my dear
Oh! my God
I'm the only one who's left alone
and go alone, my dear

He's gone
The blue water wave
and they're all over the road

and came into the rising light
and cast a shadow over the sunset
and the way to the glow
and the road with the glow of the sun

to be a burning tree
that he would be a burning tree
and go on a good day?

Oh! He's gone
but your writings remain

The sea is the mountain
everywhere you walk
with a song of poetry
and left it behind.

Korean Poetry—Love Poetry

바람의 친구

당신은 저 멀리서
사뿐히 오시는군요

푸른 솔바람으로 오세요
거치른 등걸에 기댄 채
솔 내음에 취하고 싶어요

자작나무 숲속을 지나 오세요
기다림 처럼 자작이며 서 있는
그 흰 숨결과 함께 거닐고 싶어요

강 바람으로 오세요
노을 지는 언덕에 앉아
흐르는 강물 바라보고 싶어요

넓은 벌판의 들바람
작은 풀꽃 향으로 오세요
마음껏 뛰어다니며
속 빈 마음 달래고 싶어요

지나온 길목 길목 이야기 들려주어요
두 팔 벌려 맞아줄 마지막 친구입니다

심사 뒤틀리면
때로는 광풍으로 오세요
치맛자락 날리어
맺힌 응어리 훨훨 흩어 버리겠습니다

물결 출렁이는 파도 길
금빛 찬란한 이랑 길로 오세요
벅찬 가슴이고 싶어요.

My Friend of the Wind

You are from far away
You're coming in a friendly way

Come on in the blue pine wind
Leaning against the back of his shoulder
I want to get a pine scent

Come through the birch forest
Standing on his own like a wait.
I want to walk with that white breath.

Come on to the river wind
An evening glow sitting on a hill
I want to look at the flowing river

A wide field wind
Come with a little grassy scent
Running around
I want to soothe my empty heart

Tell me about the road that you've been through.
You're the last friend I'll ever get to open my arms

If your heart hurts so much
Sometimes come like a crazy wind
My skirts flap
I'll scatter away the core.

A wave-scattering wave path
Come on down the road with the golden brilliance.
I want to be an overwhelming breasts.

꽃과 바람의 노래

권오정 지음

발 행 처 · 도서출판 청어
발 행 인 · 이영철
영   업 · 이동호
홍   보 · 천성래
기   획 · 남기환
편   집 · 방세화
디 자 인 · 이수빈 ǀ 김영은
제작이사 · 공병한
인   쇄 · 두리터

등   록 · 1999년 5월 3일
(제1999-000063호)

1판 1쇄 발행 · 2020년 4월 20일

주소 · 서울특별시 서초구 남부순환로 364길 8-15 동일빌딩 2층
대표전화 · 02-586-0477
팩시밀리 · 0303-0942-0478

홈페이지 · www.chungeobook.com
E-mail · ppi20@hanmail.net
ISBN · 979-11-5860-836-1(03810)

이 도서의 국립중앙도서관 출판시도서목록(CIP)은 서지정보유통지원시스템 홈페이지
(http://seoji.nl.go.kr)와 국가자료공동목록시스템(http://www.nl.go.kr/kolisnet)
에서 이용하실 수 있습니다.(CIP제어번호: CIP2020013650)